Jingle Bells

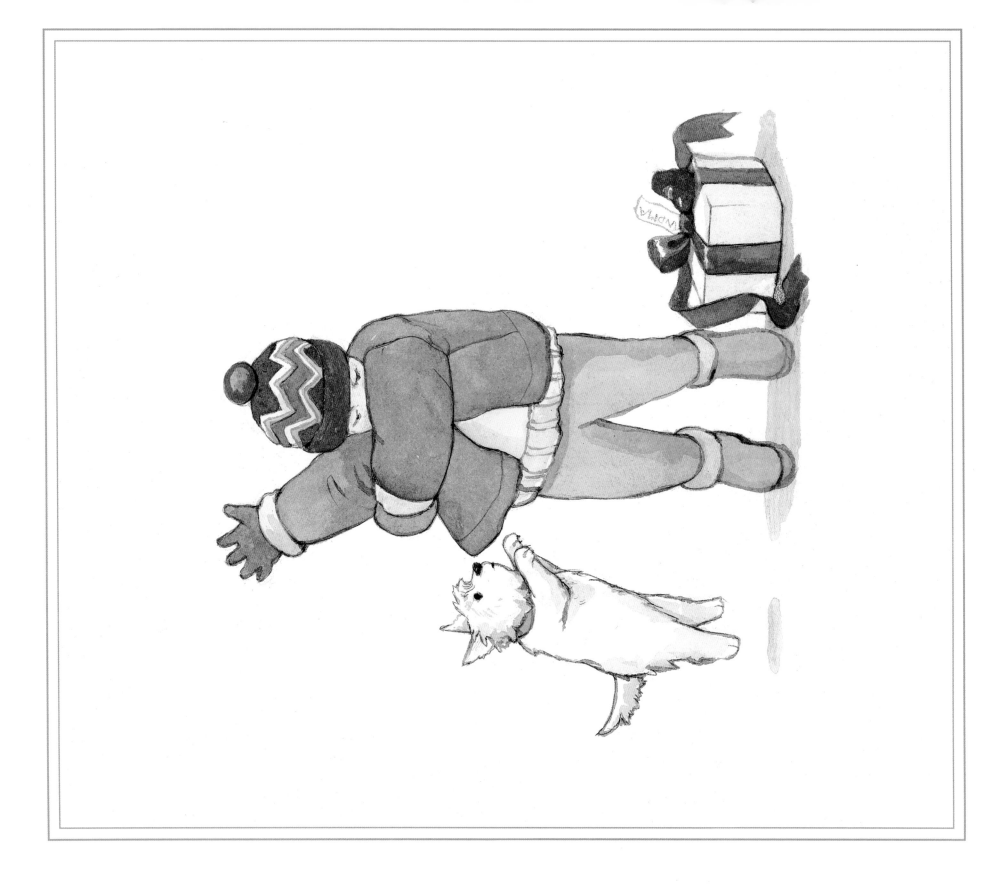

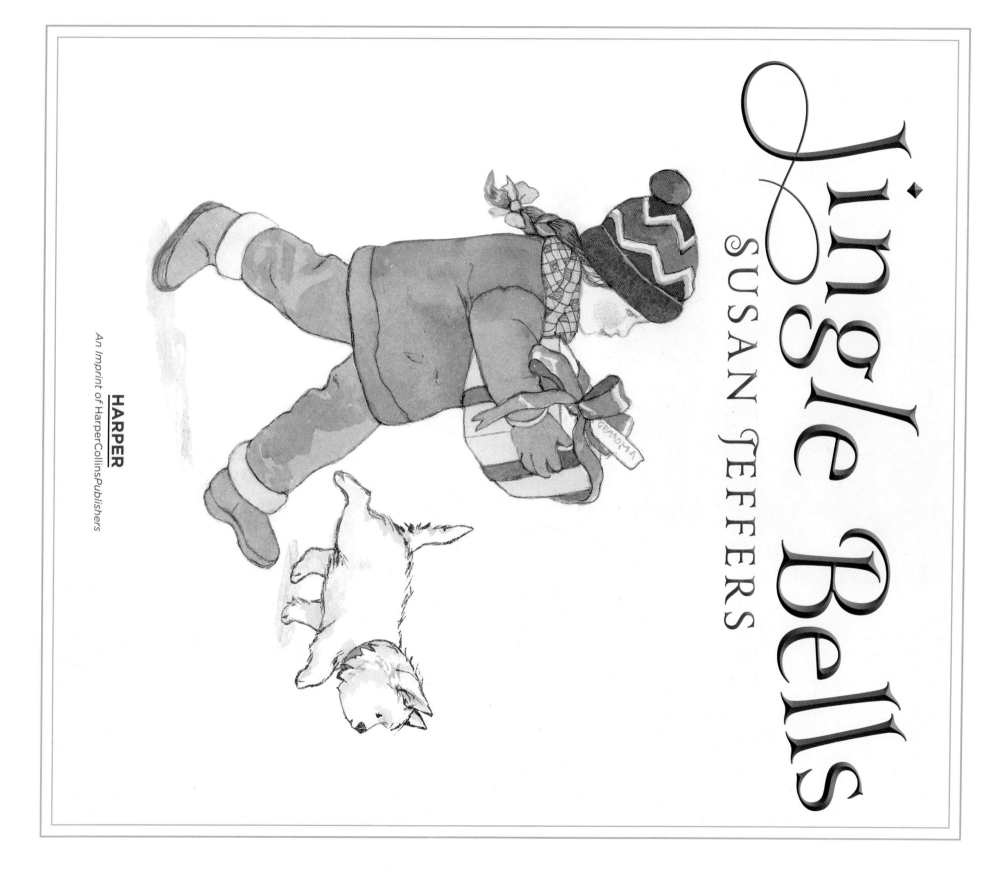

Jingle Bells

Susan Jeffers

HARPER

An Imprint of HarperCollinsPublishers

Jingle bells, jingle bells.

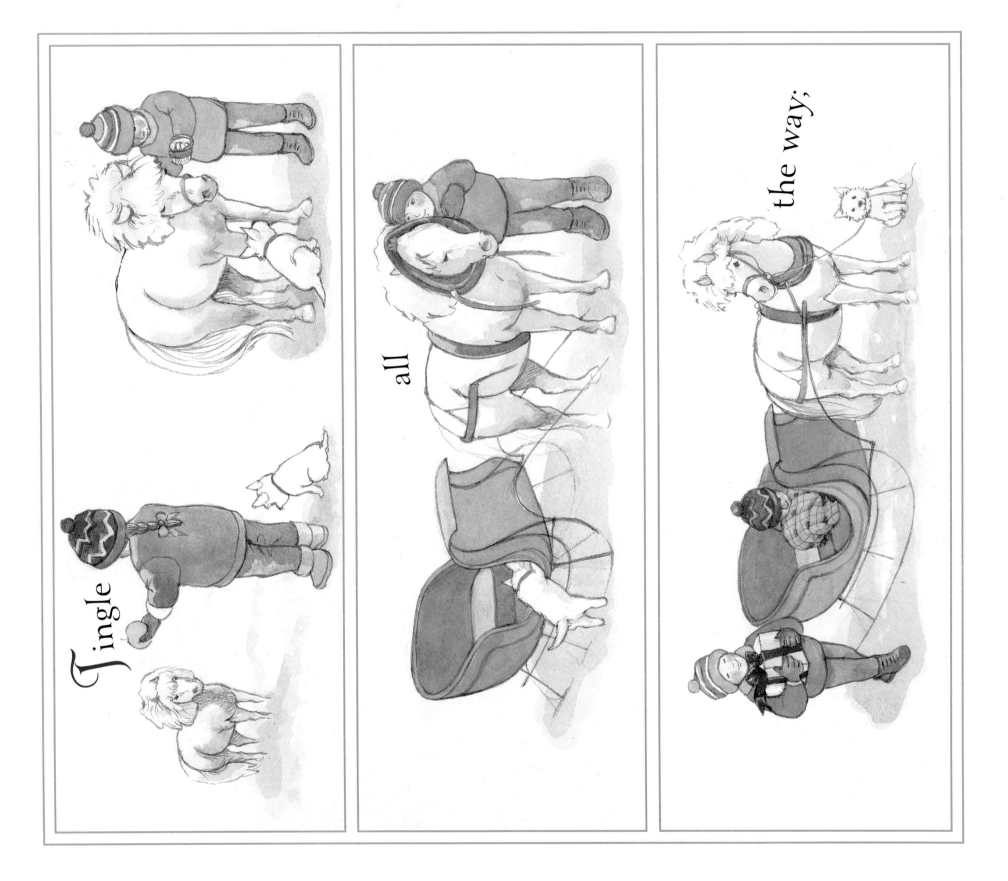

Jingle all the way;

Oh! what fun it is to ride

in a one-horse open sleigh.

Dashing through the snow,

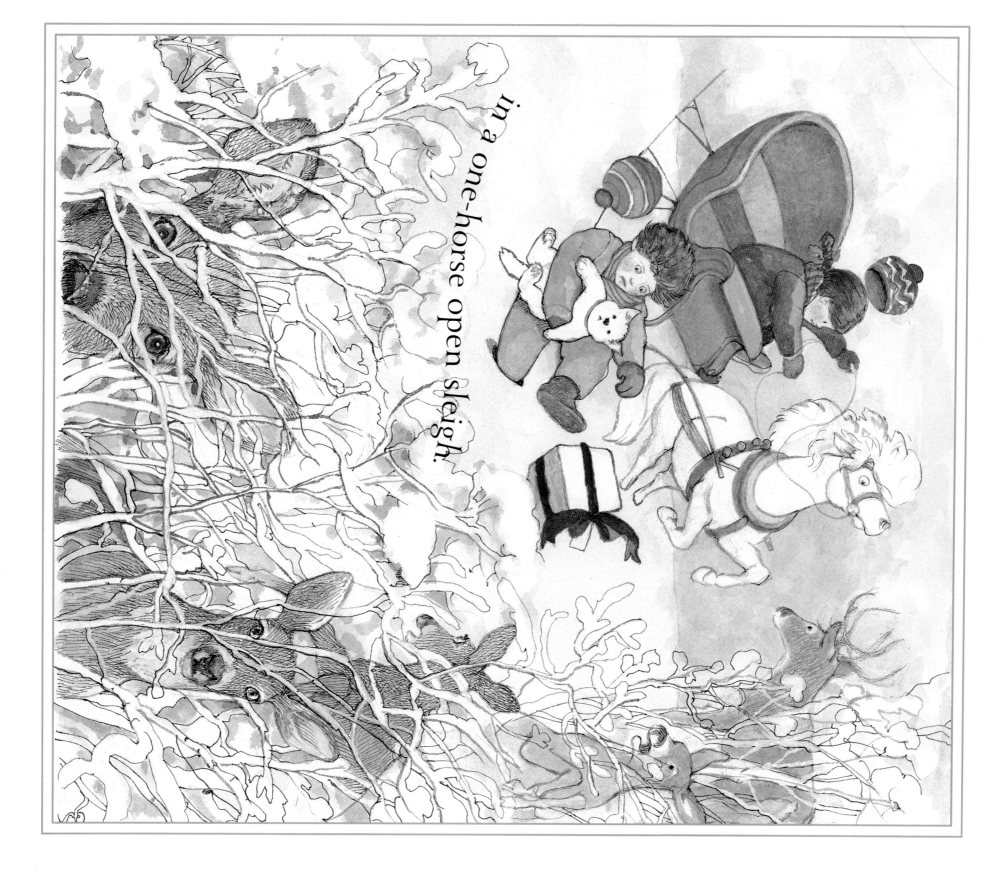

in a one-horse open sleigh.

bells on bob tail ring,

making spirits **bright,**

Oh what fun to *ride* and sing

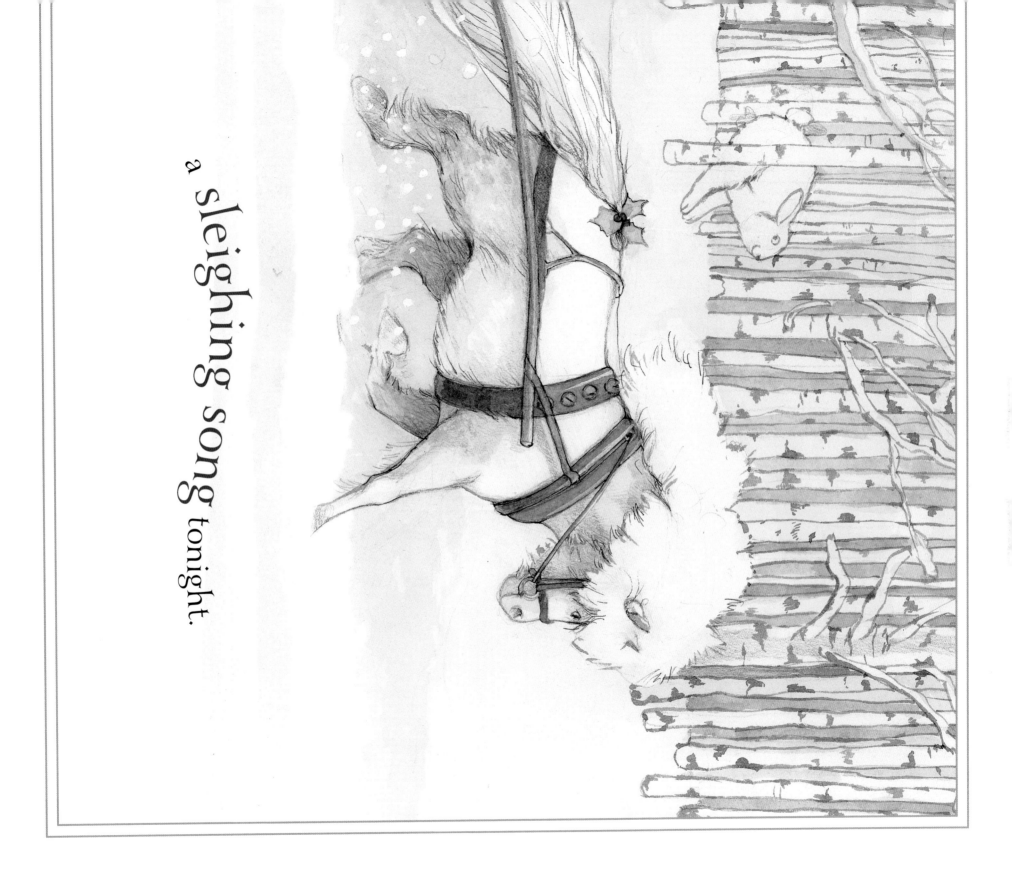

a sleighing song tonight.

Jingle bells,

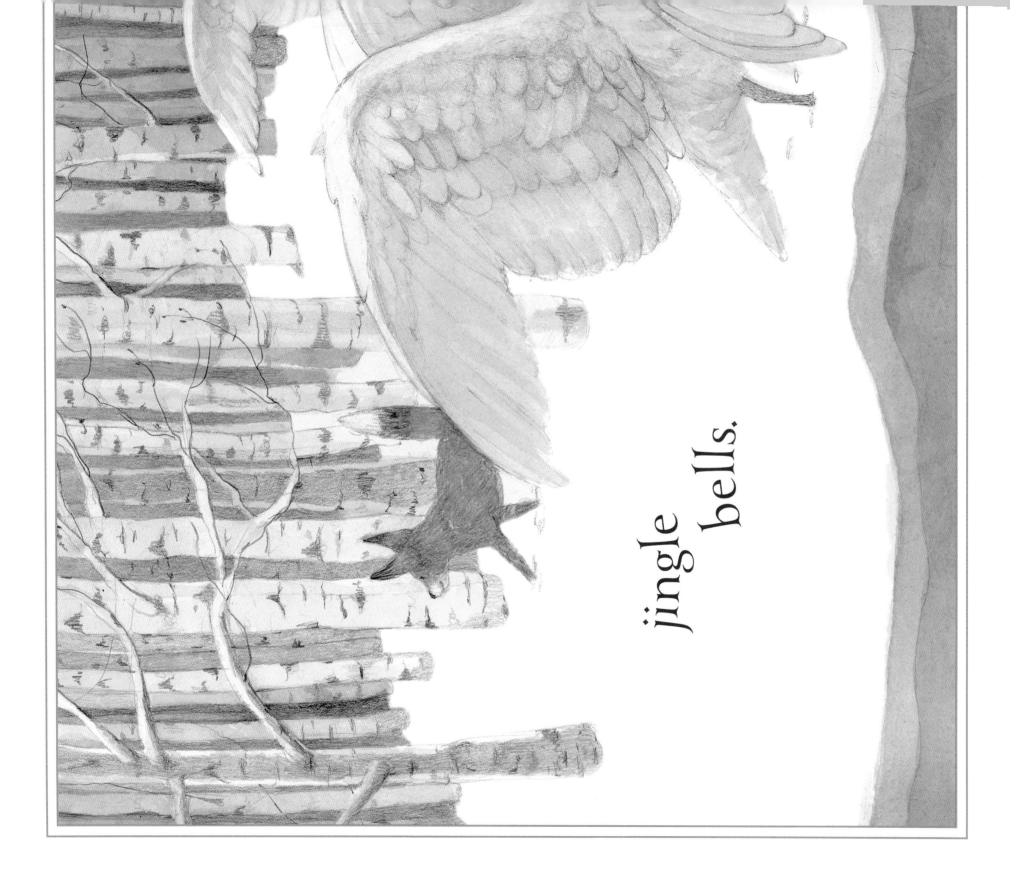

jingle bells.

all the way;

Oh! what fun
it is to ride

in a one-horse open sleigh.

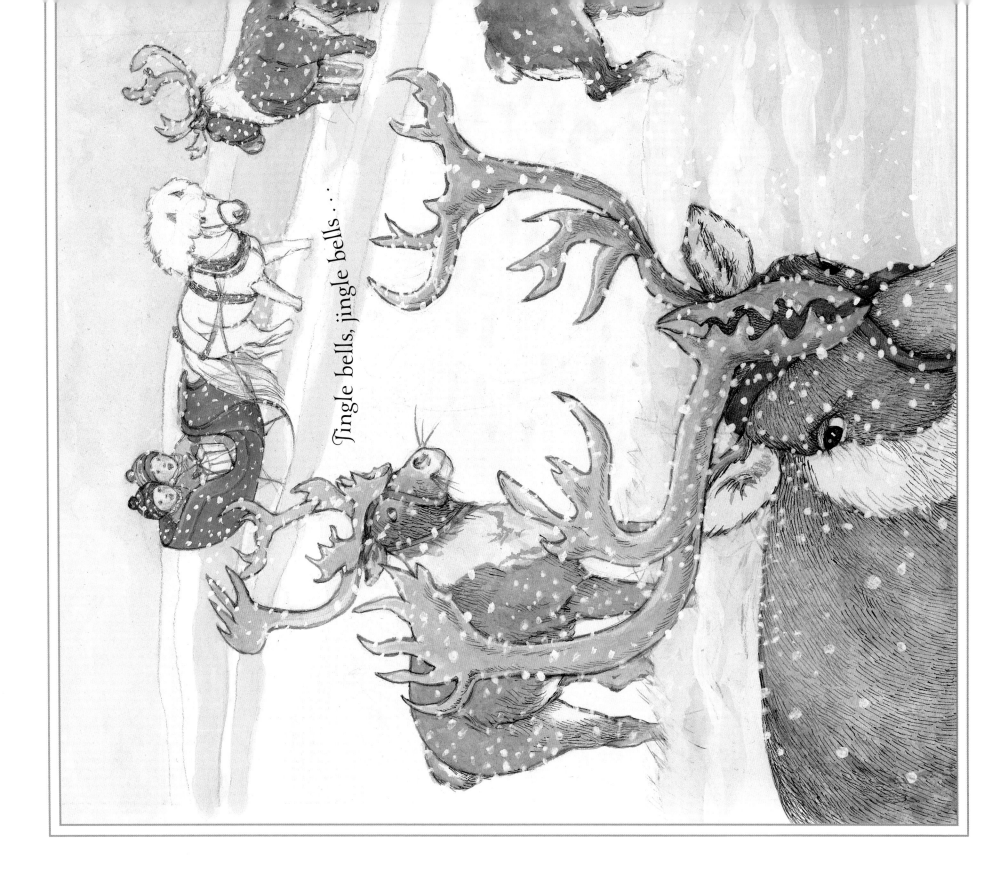

Jingle bells, jingle bells . . .

Jingle bells, jingle bells . . .

Jingle bells, jingle bells . . .

all the way!

Did you find all these winter animals?

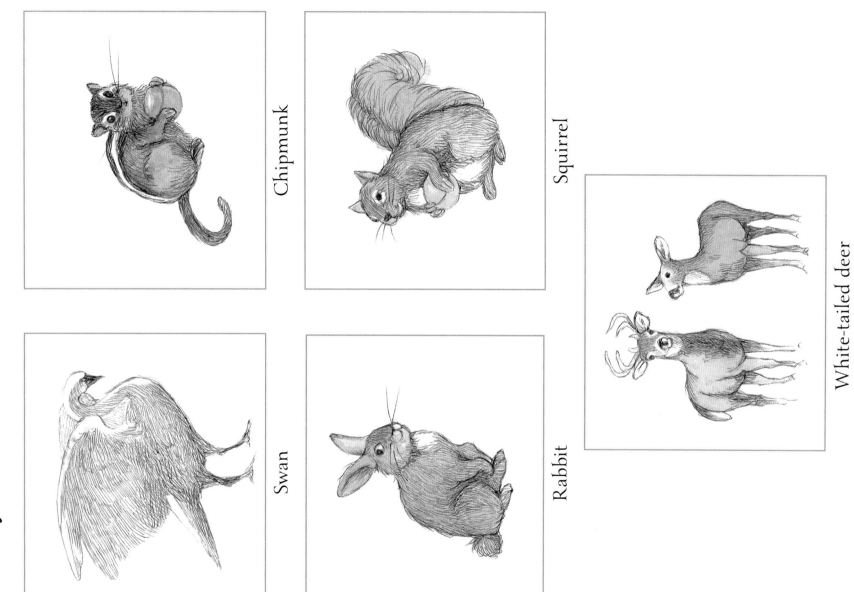

Chipmunk

Squirrel

Swan

Rabbit

White-tailed deer

Snowy owl

Raccoon

Red fox

Mouse

River otter

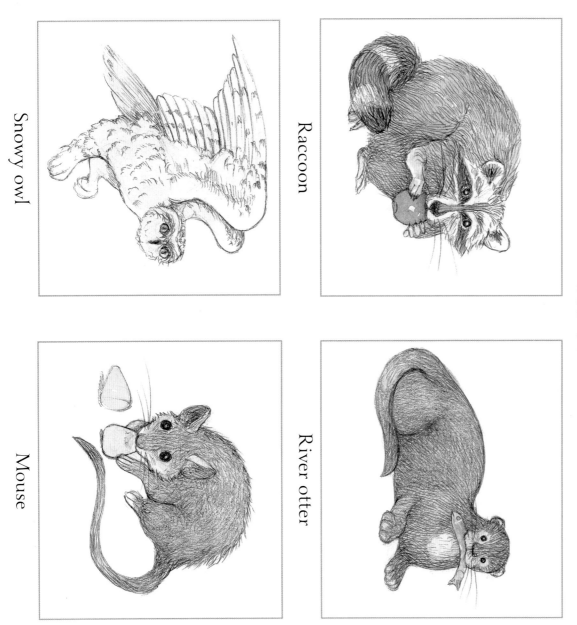

For my dear friends Liz Truly and Reno Turtur
who are always ready for a new adventure.

For my daughter, Ali Phillips, her husband, Chad, my grandchildren,
Macie and Graham, and their Baby Brother, who is on the way.

For my extraordinary painting teacher Kirill Doron.

And of course for McCloud, the star of this book.

HarperCollins
PUBLISHERS
Since 1817

Jingle Bells
Copyright © 2017 by Susan Jeffers
All rights reserved. Manufactured in China.
No part of this book may be used or reproduced in any manner whatsoever without
written permission except in the case of brief quotations embodied in critical articles
and reviews. For information address HarperCollins Children's Books,
a division of HarperCollins Publishers,
195 Broadway, New York, NY 10007.
www.harpercollinschildrens.com

ISBN 978-0-06-236020-5

The artist used watercolor and ink on Arches watercolor paper
to create the illustrations for this book.
Typography by Martha Rago
17 18 19 20 21 SCP 10 9 8 7 6 5 4 3 2 1

❖

First Edition